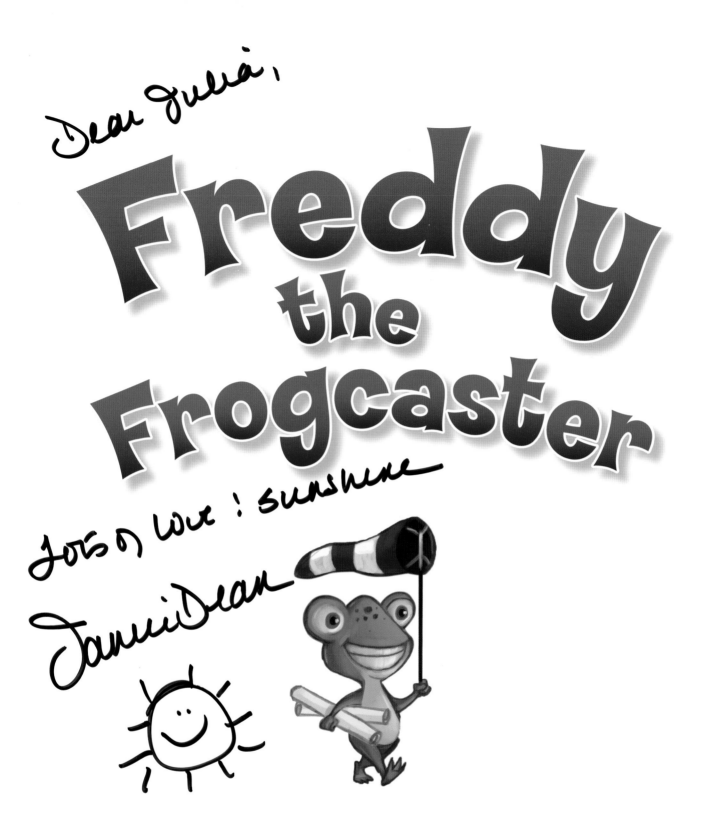

Dear Julia,

Lots of love! Sunshine

Janice Dean

Freddy the Frogcaster

By JANICE DEAN "The Weather Machine"

Illustrated by RUSS COX

Cataloging-in-Publication data on file with the Library of Congress
ISBN 978-1-62157-084-4

Published in the United States by
Regnery Kids
An imprint of Regnery Publishing, Inc.
One Massachusetts Avenue NW
Washington, DC 20001
www.Regnery.com

Manufactured in the United States of America
10 9 8 7 6 5 4 3 2

Books are available in quantity for promotional or premium use.
Write to Director of Special Sales, Regnery Publishing, Inc.,
One Massachusetts Avenue NW, Washington, DC 20001,
for information on discounts and terms, or call (202) 216-0600.

Distributed to the trade by
Perseus Distribution
250 West 57th Street
New York, NY 10107

To my beautiful boys, Matthew and Theodore.
I am so proud to be your Mama and love you both so much.
When I look at your faces, I know I am truly home.

Blue skies. Puffy white clouds. Sunshine with a light breeze.

Ahhhh…

Perfect weather for lily-pad hopping in the pond near Freddy's house.

Freddy liked rainy days too. Splashing in puddles. Listening to the pitter-patter of rain on the roof…

Snowy days were also lots of fun. A day off from school to build snowfrogs! The air so cold Freddy could see his own breath. Hot chocolate, sitting in front of a toasty fire…

All kinds of weather made Freddy happy. But what do you expect from a frog who loves weather?

Freddy's mom says Freddy was born to be a frogcaster. She remembers the very day it became clear. Freddy was hardly bigger than a tadpole as she pushed him along in his stroller.

He pointed at a big gray cloud and said, "RAIN!" It was his very first word, and he was right. Mama Frog barely had time to push the stroller home before it started pouring!

From that day on, Freddy and his mom watched Sally Croaker, the chief frogcaster, on the Frog News Network every morning. Sally was the best meteorologist in town! Everyone relied on Sally's forecasts to plan their weekends, trips, and events.

As Freddy grew, he kept his eye on the sky—watching the clouds for clues about what the weather would be like each day.

Some days there were big heaps of puffy white clouds that looked like cotton candy. Sometimes the clouds looked flat and hazy, like a big gray blanket covering the sky. Some clouds were wispy and curly—like a horse's tail!

Freddy was so interested in weather that Papa Frog built him a weather station in their backyard. It had thermometers, barometers, and all kinds of weather gear. On the roof was a weather vane to show the wind's direction.

Freddy's parents never had to ask him what he wanted for his birthday or special holidays. The weather books, charts, and tools they gave him always made him happy.

Freddy started each day by gathering weather clues. He watched the clouds, of course. But he also paid attention to clues like temperature, barometric pressure, and humidity, too. Then he ran back to the house to watch Sally's weather forecast to see if his predictions were right.

At first Freddy's mom thought all his weather watching was cute. But Freddy was right so many times that Mama Frog couldn't help but boast to her friends about Freddy's amazing weather-prediction abilities.

Before long, the whole town knew about Freddy's frogcasting ways.

One day at school, Freddy's friend, Holly Hopper, was worried that it would rain on her birthday and ruin her outdoor party.

Their teacher, Mrs. Fibian, said, "Why don't we ask our very own frogcaster for help?" Mrs. Fibian handed Freddy her chalk, and Freddy drew the forecast on the blackboard.

Forecast:
Sunny & Warm
Light wind
next few days

Lilypad pool

Lilypad School

H

He explained how a "high pressure" system was hovering right over Lilypad. This meant the weather should be sunny and warm for the next few days.

Hurray! The whole class clapped and cheered when Freddy finished his report. He was so excited and very happy when Holly invited him to her party!

sun

Holly's house

Then one day, something happened that changed Freddy's daily weather routine. Sally Croaker, Freddy's favorite TV frogcaster, had three little tadpoles! While Sally was out on tadpole leave, the Frog News Network hired a new frogcaster to fill in.

Her name was Polly Woggins, and boy oh boy, was she a hit! Every group in town invited her to come speak at their meetings—from the Salamander Society and Leaping Lizard League to the Frogmasons and the Bullfrog Ballet.

All of her special appearances kept her hopping from dawn to dusk!

All that attention was great for the News Network. Even more frogs tuned in to see the new frogcaster in action.

But Freddy started to notice a change in the forecasts. It seemed like Polly was so busy making all her celebrity appearances that she didn't have time to watch for weather clues. Several days in a row, Freddy's forecasts were more accurate than Polly's!

Some days, Polly didn't seem to have a forecast at all!

"Mother Nature is being tricky today. It may be sunny or it may rain. Who knows, it might even snow. Be prepared!"

Frogs were hopping around town juggling their umbrellas, sunglasses, and mittens. That way, they'd be prepared for any type of weather.

One day, the mayor dropped by to pay Freddy a visit. He knew about Freddy's frogcasting skills and needed a big favor.

"Mr. Mayor, what can I do for you, sir?" Freddy asked politely.

"As you know, Freddy, the Leapfrog Picnic is just a week away. It's a big event for frog families near and far. It is very important to have an accurate weather forecast that day," the mayor said.

"Why are you telling me?" Freddy looked puzzled. "Polly Woggins is the new frogcaster."

The mayor looked one way. Then he looked the other way. He leaned in close and said in a quiet voice, "The thing is, Polly is so busy with her frog fans, she barely has time to say 'weather,' let alone forecast it. I need you to keep an eye on the weather so we can plan a great day."

"I'll do my best, Mr. Mayor," Freddy said. Then Freddy offered to show the mayor his weather station.

You are invited to the Leapfrog Picnic

As Freddy led the mayor out to the backyard, he explained, "Weather gets tricky to forecast this time of year. One day it's warm and dry; the next it's cool and rainy. If it gets cold enough, it could even snow!"

The mayor was quite impressed with Freddy's weather station. "Amazing," he declared, certain he had found the right frog for the job. "Remember, Freddy, the whole town is counting on you to get this right."

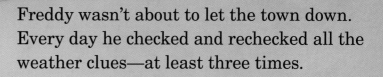

Freddy wasn't about to let the town down. Every day he checked and rechecked all the weather clues—at least three times.

Things were looking fine until the day before the picnic. If the cold front moving in from the west mixed with warm air blowing in from the south, it could bring fierce thunderstorms.

Freddy knew thunderstorms and picnics were not a good combination—and not just because it would soak all the fried cricket sandwiches! It could put the frogs in real danger.

Freddy was worried. Polly Woggins hadn't mentioned a word about rain in her last report.

Freddy had to do something! He called the mayor and asked him to meet at his weather station.

But when the mayor arrived, he wasn't alone. Freddy's favorite TV frogcaster Sally Croaker was with him—tadpoles in tow!

"I heard you needed a little help," she explained. With no time to waste, Sally and Freddy started checking for clues about that cold front coming their way.

"Mr. Mayor," she finally said. "Freddy is right. There is a big storm on the way."

"Quick! Turn on the TV," said the mayor. "Maybe we can get word to Polly in time for her last forecast."

But they were too late.

Polly was signing off, promising her viewers, "Be prepared for perfect picnic weather tomorrow!"

"Uh-oh," said Sally.

"Uh-oh is right," said the mayor.

"Hey! Wait a minute," said Freddy. "She's not all wrong."

The mayor and Sally were confused.

"Be prepared," said Freddy. "She said, 'Be prepared.' We can do that."

"Why, yes, we can," agreed the mayor, with a big sigh of relief. "Come on, Freddy, we've got work to do."

The big day started out fine—sunny and warm. All the frogs were playing and laughing, diving into the lily pond and drying off in the warm sun.

Right before lunch, things started to change. The fluffy white clouds turned gray and lumpy. There was a chill in the air, and the wind started to howl. A loud rumble sounded in the distance. Big, sloppy raindrops began to fall.

The mayor grabbed a megaphone and said, "Please move your family and your food to the Frogatorium. I repeat, everyone head to the Frogatorium now!"

Freddy held up a big white sign with a red arrow pointing the fleeing froggies in the right direction. Thanks to Sally, and a big supply of umbrellas, everyone scurried to safety.

In no time at all, the frogs were enjoying an indoor picnic—cheering on the winner of the fly-eating contest and practicing for the leapfrog race. Happy frogs were nibbling on food piled high on the big tables that Freddy, Sally, and the mayor had set up the night before. They had taken Polly's advice to "be prepared" and were ready for sunshine or rain.

Wouldn't you know it? The Leapfrog Picnic was a huge success!

The mayor and Sally made sure everyone knew that Freddy's frogcasting had saved the day. Freddy had never received so many high fives in his life!

Even Polly Woggins stopped by to thank him. She was a little embarrassed, but happy to give credit where credit was due. "You know, Freddy," she said, "I could sure use a frogcaster like you to help out with my frogcasts. Would you like to be my assistant?"

"I WOULD! I WOULD!" Freddy couldn't help but hop up and down with excitement.

Everyone laughed.

"Oh look!" said Sally. "Look over there!" All the frogs turned to see where she was pointing.

It was the biggest, most beautiful rainbow Freddy had ever seen! Freddy smiled. Things always look better after the sun comes out. And the future sure did look bright for this little frogcaster!

Hi, Friends!

Quick! Look. Right over there, outside your window. What do you see?

Is it sunny? Cloudy? Rainy? Windy? Hot? Cold? Foggy? Snowy? All of these words describe different types of weather.

One of the best parts about weather is that it is always changing! One day it's warm, another it's cold. Some days it rains, other days it snows. It all depends on what is happening in the air, or **atmosphere**, around us.

That makes it extra fun for weather lovers like me (and you!) to look for clues and be prepared for whatever the weather brings—warm hat and mittens on a cold winter day, t-shirt and flip flops on a sunny summer day.

People who study the weather are called forecasters or **meteorologists**. Unless, of course, they are a frog like me. In that case, they are called frogcasters. We make the weather predictions you see on television, in the newspaper, online, and on the radio.

But forecasting is not guessing. Forecasters and—um—frogcasters look for weather clues and use special scientific tools to make accurate forecasts.

Clouds are one of the best weather clues out there! Plus, clouds are really cool! When water evaporates (like a puddle drying up on the sidewalk), it doesn't disappear, it moves up into the air and forms little water drops or ice crystals. When millions and millions of these little droplets get together, they become a cloud.

I love looking for clues in the clouds. Every day I look up at the sky and draw pictures of the clouds I see.

Sometimes I see white and puffy **cumulus clouds**. They remind me of cotton balls, a sheep's wool, or cotton candy. People call these "fair weather clouds" because they show up on the prettiest days with lots of blue sky behind them. If you look really closely (and use your imagination a bit), sometimes you can see the shapes of animals and other things in this type of cloud.

Other days I have to look way, way up in the sky where **cirrus clouds** gather in the super cold air. These clouds are thin, wispy, feathery, and white. Some look like a horse's tail. It kind of looks like someone has stretched the cloud out across the sky. These clouds are made of tiny ice crystals and—clue alert!—sometimes mean that a storm is on its way or coming to an end.

On bleak, gray days I find **stratus clouds**. These low-hanging clouds spread out across the sky like a dreary blanket. When you see this type of cloud in the sky, it is a clue that rain or snow may be on its way.

Watch out! **Cumulonimbus clouds** are big, towering clouds that carry all sorts of bad weather in them. These exploding "thunderstorm" clouds can contain heavy rain, lightning, thunder, hail, strong winds, and sometimes even tornadoes! When you see these types of clouds in the sky, you know it's time to go inside to a safe place.

TYPES OF CLOUDS

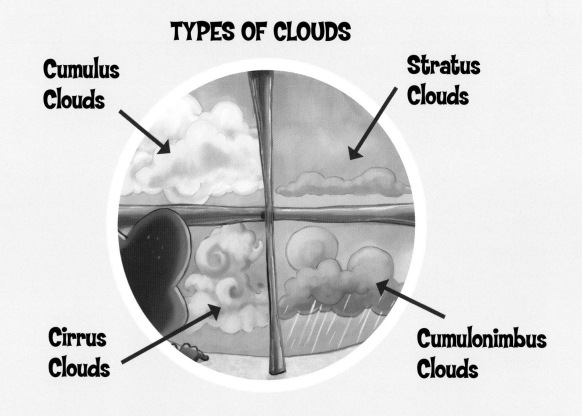

Cumulus Clouds

Stratus Clouds

Cirrus Clouds

Cumulonimbus Clouds

Of course, clouds are just one clue I look for in order to predict the weather. There are lots of tools in my weather station that I use to gather weather information. Here are a few tools I (and other forecasters) use.

A **thermometer** is a tool used to measure temperature (how hot or cold something is). The freezing point when water turns into ice is 32 degrees Fahrenheit (or 0 degrees Celsius). The higher the temperature, the hotter it is. The lower the temperature, the colder it is.

A **rain gauge** is an instrument used to measure the amount of rain that falls from the sky—it's basically a cup that catches rain drops. I put my rain gauge in an open area protected from the wind, away from trees or buildings. That way nothing gets in the way of an accurate reading. Actually, my dad and I made my rain gauge out of an empty coffee can. Once the rain falls, I just take a ruler and measure how much rain fell. Then I record it in my weather notebook with the date and time.

A **weather vane** shows the direction of the wind, whether it's blowing from the north, south, east, or west. My weather vane is attached to the roof of my weather station.

An **anemometer** is an instrument that spins like a windmill and moves faster (or slower) depending on the speed of the wind.

A **barometer** is an instrument forecasters use to measure atmospheric pressure. Finding out whether air pressure is high or low is another "clue" I use to predict the weather.

High pressure is when the air pressure rises, according to the barometer, and it means fair weather is usually on the way. When the air pressure falls, an area of **low pressure** is usually forming. You might see rain or even stormy weather very soon. Remember when I made the prediction for my friend Holly Hopper's birthday party? The map I drew on the blackboard had a big "H" on it, which meant clear skies or good weather was heading our way. If a storm were coming, I would have used an "L" to show a low-pressure system.

What's on a Weather Map?

First, let's talk about an **air mass**. A big area of weather that has the same composition throughout is called an air mass. You can have a cold air mass and a warm air mass. In between air masses, you have a "front," which is like a divider or line that separates one air mass from the other.

Cold front: this line on a map (shown in blue) shows you where the leading edge of a cold air mass is moving in.

Warm front: this line on the map (shown in red) shows you where the leading edge of a warm air mass is pushing through.

Radar is a very important tool used by weather forecasters on television to show viewers when precipitation is moving into their area.

Speaking of **precipitation**, this is a fancy word for any type of water that falls from the sky. It includes rain, freezing rain, sleet, snow, or hail.

By the Way...

Have you ever wondered how **rain** forms? Well, rain happens inside of the clouds. If the clouds are big enough and have enough water droplets, the droplets stick together and form even bigger drops. If the drops get heavy enough, they fall to the ground as rain.

Snow works just like rain, except, when it is really cold, snow crystals form from tiny raindrops inside the cloud. When the crystals stick together, they become snowflakes, and when the snowflakes get heavy enough, they fall from the sky. Although every snowflake that falls from the clouds has six sides, each flake is different! Each tiny flake is a piece of nature's artwork!

In a **thunderstorm cloud**, the air is moving very quickly with strong, sudden movements. Because of this turbulence, lots of tiny drops of water and ice bump into each other at very fast speeds. This rapid motion causes positive and negative charges to build up, and this makes electricity. When enough electricity builds up, it bursts and flashes. This is called **lightning**.

Lightning is very hot—five times hotter than the sun's surface! It's so hot that it heats the cooler air around it and makes a loud BOOM you hear called **thunder**. Thunderstorms can produce a lot of rain, and even severe weather, too, such as hail, strong damaging winds, and sometimes tornadoes.

When sunlight shines through drops of rain, the light breaks up into colors and a **rainbow** appears in the sky. You can't touch rainbows. They are an illusion of the light from the sky.

Wind is air in motion. Wind occurs when warm air moves up into the atmosphere and cool air moves in to replace it. Warm and cool temperatures affect wind speed and direction.

Predicting the weather is just one of a meteorologist's jobs. Warning people when the weather could turn bad and cause problems is another big part of their job. Just like in the story, a bad weather advisory helps people "be prepared!"

Hey, you know what? You can be a frog…I mean forecaster, too. All you need is a notebook and a pencil or pen to start recording all the weather clues you can find each day. Some of these clues you can find just by looking at the sky and walking outside to see if it is warm or cold. Other clues you can find online at your favorite weather website or by watching weather forecasts on television.

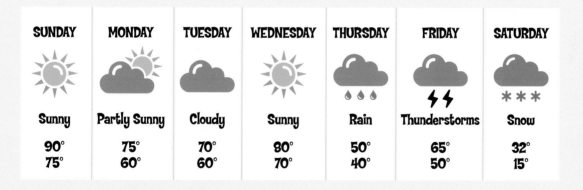

SUNDAY	MONDAY	TUESDAY	WEDNESDAY	THURSDAY	FRIDAY	SATURDAY
Sunny	Partly Sunny	Cloudy	Sunny	Rain	Thunderstorms	Snow
90°	75°	70°	80°	50°	65°	32°
75°	60°	60°	70°	40°	50°	15°

Of course, if you really want to hop into weather like I do, you can set up your own weather station. Go online to our website at **www.RegneryKids.com** to find instructions on how to make your very own weather forecasting instruments. Happy forecasting!

Your weather-loving friend,

Freddy

Acknowledgments

To Roger Ailes, you gave me a dream job here at Fox. I am forever grateful.

To Peter and Cheryl Barnes, for believing in my little weather book idea.

To Chuck Leavell, for reading the first rough edit of Freddy and passing it along to Peter, despite being one of the busiest men in show business.

To Russ Cox, whose brilliant illustrations allow Freddy to "leap" off the page. And to Amanda Larsen for putting all the pieces and parts together to create this book.

To Diane Reeves, my editor, who knows how to speak "frog" fluently, brilliantly organized my thoughts, and worked tirelessly to meet deadlines.

To Jane Skinner, who listened to my Freddy idea for many years, and kept encouraging me to "write it down, already."

To Megyn Kelly and Doug Brunt, whose friendship means the world to me. Thank you for your constant support and guidance.

To Stella and Craig Dean. Thanks for always believing in me.

To Dianne Brandi, a special thanks for being so generous with my endless stream of questions, being fair, honest, and always so kind to me.

To Brandon Noriega, who pretended he was a first grader when reading my draft and put his seal of approval on my meteorological accuracy!

And finally, to my husband, Sean, I never believed in fate until we met on that midtown corner in December 2002. Thank you for filling in the piece of my heart that I was missing for so long.